The Somerset Collection

is proud to have commissioned this wonderful holiday story by local author, Matt Faulkner. We hope you read it, enjoy it and make it a part of your holiday tradition, year after year.

For my friends Budda, Bébe, Chuckie, Ramiro and J.

I wish to thank Glen and Jackie Michaels for their guidance, generosity and the best darned tuna fish sandwiches on the planet.

M.F.

Book design by Julie Pincus

 Published by The Somerset Collection Inc.
Printed in the U.S.A

The Giving Season
Written and Illustrated by
Matt Faulkner

"Good day to you. I am called Yoric. An actor by

trade, I'm the master of this fine Pageant Wagon. This motley bunch is my troop. We rove the countryside together, forever in search of an audience. Makes no difference to us if you're a Princess or a pauper, it's the roar of the crowd we crave. Of course we keep any coins that are tossed our way. After all, it would be impolite to return a gift. Which reminds me of a story....

Many years ago

my troop and I ventured into a strange land in search of a place to practice our craft. We carried with us news of a new tradition. This tradition was called The Giving Season and it came from the East. It was to be held during the dark days of winter, when even the warmest of hearts can turn cold and gray. The tradition called for candles to be lit, songs to be sung, and most of all, for gifts to be given. Where ever the Giving Season was celebrated it left the folk feeling wondrously happy.

traveling we found ourselves knocking upon the front gate of a meager little castle. The people within were a sour faced bunch and we soon saw the reason why. In the whole place there was not a single child! For well over twenty years there had been only one baby born in all the kingdom. Her name was Sophie and she was the daughter of the King and Queen. She had grown to be a lovely child, yet for all her sweetness, Sophie was considered a great bother by the townsfolk. Even her parents found her irksome. Everyone had become so grown-up that they had no use for the playful little Princess. So they kept her locked up in one of the castles towers. She was well fed and had no lack of toys. Yet Sophie spent most of her days staring down at the people below and wishing for a friend.

Of all the odd

people who lived in the castle there was none odder than Phelonious Quirk. Phelonious was the King's Court Jester. He was very good at his job and was known through out the land for his ability to make things disappear.

In the days leading

up to the celebration, the jester spent all of his time spying on people as they made and wrapped their gifts. For some reason known only to Phelonious, he had begun to believe that all these gifts were meant for him alone. It was this misunderstanding that was to be the start of a great deal of trouble.

When the morning of the

Giving Season finally dawned, Phelonious was the first to arrive in the great hall. The King rose and gave a long speech on the true meaning of the Season, yet the Jester heard not a word. He was too excited to pay attention to anything but the great pile of presents. He watched as the King took the first gift from the pile of goodies and gave it to the Queen. Phelonious was dumbstruck as he watched the Queen tear open the present and pull out a pair of diamond studded, ruby inlaid ear muffs.

As the Queen placed the gift upon her head, Phelonious made his move. Performing a splendid triple somersault, he vaulted across the hall and landed betwixt the King and Queen. "Excuse me, Your Highness, but these are mine." he said and politely plucked the muffs from the Queen's ears. He then vaulted back across the room where he came to rest atop the pile of gifts.

A stunned

silence hung over the hall "I want my ear-muffs!" bellowed the Queen. The King shook his fist at the Jester. "Quirk, come down here at once!" Hoping that he was as yet the brunt of some horrible prank, Phelonious playfully placed the muffs on his own head and cried "If you want 'em so bad, then come up and get 'em." The King scrambled from his throne and promptly fell to the floor. "You've gone too far this time, Quirk." he growled. "Guards! Arrest that fool!"

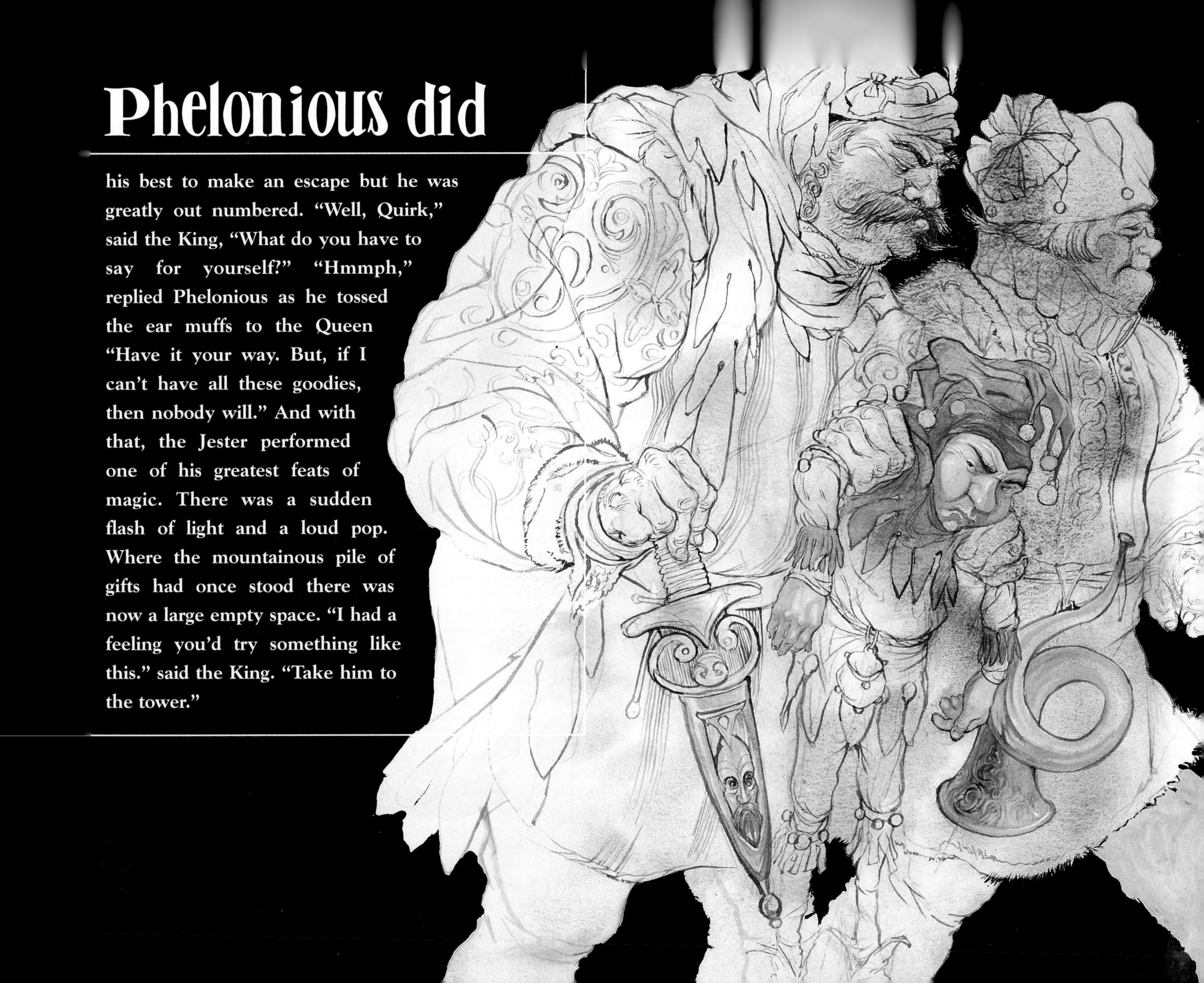

Phelonious did

his best to make an escape but he was greatly out numbered. "Well, Quirk," said the King, "What do you have to say for yourself?" "Hmmph," replied Phelonious as he tossed the ear muffs to the Queen "Have it your way. But, if I can't have all these goodies, then nobody will." And with that, the Jester performed one of his greatest feats of magic. There was a sudden flash of light and a loud pop. Where the mountainous pile of gifts had once stood there was now a large empty space. "I had a feeling you'd try something like this." said the King. "Take him to the tower."

For all his flipping

through the air, Phelonious had a horrible fear of heights. The first few hours spent in the tower were very difficult for him. He couldn't believe his eyes when he saw a little girl hop through his open window. "Hello." she said, "My name is Sophie. What's yours?"

Phelonious stared in wide eyed wonder as Sophie placed a tiny box in his hands. "Go ahead and open it." she said "It's a little something from me to you. So we can be friends." The Jester soon found his wits and rudely tore open the box. Inside there was an egg. "Blue birds come each spring and nest around my window." said Sophie. "This egg didn't hatch so I kept it for a special occasion."

"Hmmph" snorted

Phelonious as he tossed the box back at her. "That's all right." replied the Princess as she climbed back out of the window. "I know just how you feel." Phelonious stood to see Sophie walking across a delicate bridge that linked her tower to his. "Just yell if you need anything." she cried and climbed back into her window.

Phelonious spent a

cold night in his drafty tower. He was awakened early the next morning by the King's counselors. "The King would like to know," they inquired "if you are ready to make the gifts reappear?" "Hmmph." he replied. The counselors made a hasty exit. Shortly thereafter, a small bowl of porridge was slid under his door. "Eat slowly, Jester." said a voice on the other side, "That's all you'll be getting today."

When Phelonious had

licked his bowl clean for the third time he was surprised to see Sophie climbing through his window. She held in her hands a silver platter piled high with pancakes and sausage. Placing the platter before him, she said "I hope you're hungry. They always give me too much." Phelonious didn't wait for her to finish. Clutching sausages in both hands, he dove face first into the hot cakes.

The platter was soon empty. Phelonious sat back and twiddled his thumbs. All this kindness was making him very perplexed. "Hmmph." he said. "Why are you being so nice to me?" Sophie picked up the empty platter. "We're neighbors." she said as she climbed out the window. "Why shouldn't we be friendly?" Phelonious was flabbergasted. It was all he could do to sit and stare out at the blue sky.

Sophie soon returned.

She was carrying an assortment of objects. There were birds nests and feathers, some more blue birds eggs, an old kite and some tattered ribbons. “My parents are always sending me stuff to keep me busy. All sorts of dolls and toys and crazy gadgets. But these are the things I love to play with.” One by one, she handed the fragile pieces to Phelonious. Each one had a story. Phelonious listened intently. For the moment all his worries were forgotten. When they had gone over each of Sophie’s prized possessions, Phelonious performed some simple magic. Sophie was very impressed. In this way, the day flew by.

By the time the

sun was setting, Phelonious and Sophie had become friends. This was something new for the both of them as neither one had ever had a friend before. They shook hands and promised to do it all over again tomorrow. When Sophie climbed onto the window sill she noticed that the wind had picked up. “You’ll need a blanket tonight.” she said. “I’ll be right back.” Phelonious walked to the window and watched his friend make her way across the stone parapet.

When Sophie climbed

back out of her tower, she was carrying a large blanket. The wind was blowing fiercely and she made her way carefully across the slender bridge. Phelonious gasped when he saw the wind catch Sophie and her blanket and toss them high over head. For a moment, Sophie hung in the air, both hands clinging tightly to the blanket. When the wind dropped, Sophie plunged quickly downward. Luckily, a corner of the fluttering blanket caught itself on a gargoyle's horn. Sophie held on desperately. "Phelonious!" she cried. "Help!"

Phelonious stared in

shock at his new found friend. “What to do? What to do?” he said to himself. “Hold on!” he cried. “I will help you!” For one terrible moment, he couldn’t think of a single thing to do. Just then he clapped his hands and climbed onto the window sill. ”I know!” he said “The gifts!”. Pointing down at the ground he cried:

Bring them Back
And pile them High.
Do it Now
And don’t be Shy.

One by one, the

gifts that had been taken from the great hall reappeared. Stacked one on top of the other, the pile of goodies climbed the tower wall. Phelonious laughed with glee. But his laughter was soon cut short. The pile of gifts came to a halt far below where Sophie was hanging. Once again, Phelonious had to think quickly. "Aha!" he cried "The King!" He ran to his door and banged on it. "What do you want?" said a voice on the other side. "Tell the King to look in the court yard! His goodies have been returned!" The only reply was the sound of scampering feet as they rushed down the narrow tower stairway.

Phelonious ran back

to his window. Sophie was still holding tight to her blanket. Far below, the King and Queen had rushed outside to find the gifts piled against the tower. The courtyard was filled with cheering townsfolk. A cry rose up from the crowd as someone pointed out the tiny figure hanging from the blanket above. No time was wasted. Quickly, they climbed the brightly wrapped gifts. When they reached the top of the pile, they climbed on top of each others shoulders. Once again, it looked as if Sophie would be saved. But when the last man had climbed atop the teetering pile of people and presents, he found himself just short of their goal.

"Not again!" cried

Phelonious. There was but one thing left for the Jester to do. Gulping back his fear, he climbed out onto the stone parapet. The wind tore at him. His knees shook. Ever so slowly, Phelonious crawled across the perilous bridge until finally, with a sigh of relief, he pressed himself tightly against Sophie's tower. "Hold on!" he shouted. "I'm coming!" Hand over hand, he climbed down the craggy stone work until he was sitting atop the gargoyle that held the corner of Sophie's blanket. With great care, he loosened the cloth from it's hold and lowered Sophie into the arms of the topmost townsman. Through the howling wind he could hear the cheers of the people below.

And so, we have

nearly come to the end of our story. All that's left to say is that most everything turned out well. As soon as everyone was safely down upon the ground, they tore into the pile of gifts. Hardly anyone was displeased with the goodies they received and almost everyone was pleasantly baffled by this new sensation called The Joy of Giving.

After the shock of seeing Sophie dangling high over head, the King and Queen realized how terribly selfish they had been in sticking her up in the tower and promised never to do it again.

Sophie soon forgot her hair raising experience, yet she would always remember Phelonious Quirk, her first true friend.

In time,

Phelonious was pardoned by the King, who was most grateful to the Jester for saving his daughter's life. Phelonious decided to turn over a new leaf and returned all of the things which he'd at one time or another made disappear. All, that is, except the diamond studded, ruby inlaid ear muffs. No one is quite sure whose ears those muffs are warming.

THE END